The Fairly OddParents!
NICKELODEON

TIMMY TURNER'S

TOP-SECRET

NOTEBOOK

by ERICA PASS and
TIMMY TURNER

illustrated by PIERO PILUSO

Simon Spotlight/Nickelodeon
New York   London   Toronto   Sydney   Singapore

D0474222

Butch Hartman

Based on the TV show The Fairly OddParents® created by Butch Hartman as seen on Nickelodeon®

SIMON SPOTLIGHT
An imprint of Simon & Schuster Children's Publishing Division
1230 Avenue of the Americas, New York, New York 10020

Copyright © 2004 Viacom International Inc. All rights reserved. NICKELODEON, The Fairly OddParents, and all related titles, logos, and characters are trademarks of Viacom International Inc.

All rights reserved, including the right of reproduction in whole or in part in any form. SIMON SPOTLIGHT and colophon are registered trademarks of Simon & Schuster.

Book design by James Salerno

Manufactured in the United States of America
First Edition
10 9 8 7 6 5 4 3 2 1
ISBN 0-689-86325-X

Hey! What are you doing snooping around? Are you looking for my top-secret notebook—the ultracool one that's all about my . . . uh, wait. . . . I mean the one that is absolutely NOT at all about my fairy godparents? You know, the one that says "Stay Out! That means you, Vicky and Mr. Crocker!" on the cover? Well, you won't find it here. Believe me, it's pretty hidden. You don't expect me to leave something like that just lying around for anyone to see, do you?

STAY OUT!

Before I let you in on where my secret notebook is, you have to promise that you WON'T TELL ANYONE!!! I don't even want to think about what could happen if my notebook fell into the wrong hands—it would be a total mega-disaster! The kind that means no more Cosmo and Wanda! Who are Cosmo and Wanda, you ask? Well, if you promise not to tell ANYONE what I'm about to tell you, stay tuned and you'll find out! Promise? Okay.

My top-secret notebook is really hard to find. No one except for me, Cosmo, and Wanda knows where it is, and even we have trouble finding it. This is what you have to do to get to the notebook:

OK, you found it. If you haven't already guessed, you can never be too careful around here. People would totally flip out if they knew that I had–shhh!–fairy godparents.

There have already been too many close calls!

But I know one thing for sure–my life has never been the same since Cosmo and Wanda showed up. She put the 'wand' in Wanda and he . . . well, he helps too!

POOF!

Here's a little history . . .
okay, NOW, guys!

Thanks, Timmy! It all started one day
when Timmy's baby-sitter—

ICKY!

He *means* Vicky. (Although she *is* quite icky.)
Anyway, one night when she was being her normal, evil self—

—inflicting cruelty on poor Timmy—

—we sensed that Timmy Turner needed
a pair of very special fairy godparents—

US!

We come from Fairy World—

More on that later!

—and have to report back
to our boss, Jorgen—

More on him later!

—but our main reason
for sticking around is
so we can help Timmy
whenever he needs it!
Although there *are*
some rules . . . If we
don't follow Da Rules,
we could be sent back
to Fairy World, and
Timmy would have to
make do without his
favorite fairies.

The most important rule
is that a kid actually has to
say "I wish" for any wish to
be granted.

And sometimes I like to get creative!

THESE ARE THE BIGGEST RULES OF DA RULES:

RuLe #1:
FAIRY GODPARENTS
ONLY GRANT WISHES
TO KIDS.

RuLe #2:
A KID WITH FAIRY
GODPARENTS CAN'T TELL
ANYONE THEY EXIST.

Rule #3: FAIRY GODPARENTS CAN'T EVER INTERFERE WITH TRUE LOVE—EVEN WHEN IT'S TRUE LOVE BETWEEN A SLIMY ALIEN PRINCE AND YOUR GROSS BABY-SITTER.

POOF!

He was yummy!

Being a fairy godparent is harder than it looks. Hey, Cosmo, how about the time Timmy wished that he was our fairy godparent? I thought he'd never get the goldfish thing down!

That was funny!

Okay! Back to business!

So *that's* Cosmo and Wanda. For the most part, they do an awesome job with the wishes—they've switched me into a dog, and sent me back in time, and into space, and into my favorite comic book!

YUCK!

But sometimes things don't go *exactly* as planned . . .

Like the time I wished to switch places with Vicky so she became a little kid and I became her baby-sitter. But then Cosmo and Wanda had to become *her* fairy godparents.

Or the time I wished that everyone looked alike, so no one would tease people who were different. But then none of the fairy godparents could find their kids, so they couldn't grant wishes anymore. It caused a magical backup and fairies were exploding all over the place!

Or the time I wished for an alien, so my friends A.J. and Chester would be impressed, and Cosmo and Wanda summoned Mark, this alien prince from some planet named Yugopatamia, who ended up falling in love with Vicky. Then his alien parents said they'd destroy Earth if Mark didn't come home, but he wouldn't leave since he loved Vicky so much and. . . . Well, I guess you had to be there, but it was a prime example of a good wish gone bad!

I'm not the only one around here who gets turned into things. Cosmo and Wanda have to cover their tracks all the time! They can turn themselves into just about anything! They've been pencils . . . and pets . . . and flowers . . . and fruit . . . and butterflies . . .

Ooh, butterflies! I *love* butterflies!

But usually when they're not their fairy selves, they take the form of goldfish in a bowl in my room.

Timmy may be the only kid in town with fish that can grant him wishes!

I love goldfish!

Just call us wish fish!

They're the best pets I've ever had! So you might be wondering, just where do Cosmo and Wanda come from? Well, it's this place called FAIRY WORLD. They used to train with other fairy godparents at the Fairy Academy under this really big, muscle-y dude named Jorgen von Strangle. Boy, is he tough.

Even his muscles have muscles!

He's sort of our boss, though, so we have to pay attention to what he says.

Even when he says silly, made-up scary things like, "You two have caused a major magical fluctuation in the magic space continuum flux!"

But Cosmo, we *have* caused major magical fluctuations in the magic space continuum flux.

Huh? Oh, well, um . . . chocolate snake!

Even with all the mishaps Cosmo and Wanda definitely make life easier! But my life isn't perfect! There's always (shudder) . . . Vicky. Vicky's my baby-sitter. She lives to make my life miserable.

Look what I found just last week when Vicky was yelling at me to wash her dishes and do her laundry and iron her socks. *This* fell out of her pocket:

1001 WAYS TO TORTURE POOR INNOCENT CHILDREN AND MILK THEIR MOMS AND DADS FOR CASH WHILE CONVINCING THEM I AM SWEET AND NICE

But I guess I have to be grateful to Vicky in some strange way, 'cause without her, I might never have met Cosmo and Wanda!

Tootie, Vicky's younger sister, likes to bug me too, but in a different way. She's always running after me and trying to kiss me and stuff. It's totally gross! But then I found out that Vicky tortures her just as much as she tortures me. And I realized that, well, I guess Tootie's not so bad . . . but don't let anyone know I said that.

There's someone else who's always hot on my trail, but I don't think he likes me as much as Tootie does. My teacher, Mr. Crocker, is obsessed with exposing fairy godparents! He's totally onto us. So far we've managed to keep one step ahead of him, but there have been lots of close calls.

Like the time I needed a show-and-tell project, and Cosmo and Wanda got me a real live dinosaur!

And the time Francis wanted to beat me up, and Cosmo and Wanda made me invisible. I felt invincible when I was invisible!

Luckily, Crocker's not so good at actually catching anyone. Still, I gotta steer clear of him, and keep Cosmo and Wanda under fairy wraps.

Speaking of obstacles at school . . . Francis is this bully whose favorite hobby is to pound me and the other kids. (Too bad they don't all have their own Cosmos and Wandas!) Francis may not be the brightest bulb in the socket, but he is big. And he enjoys crushing anyone who is smaller than he is.

Francis

Me

It's a good thing I have friends at school to back me up. My best friends, A.J. and Chester, are awesome! We play video games together, hate Vicky together, worship Crash Nebula together . . . I also worship Trixie Tang, this superpopular girl. I think she just may have a little crush on me, too! But A.J. and Chester always say, "Dude, she doesn't even know you exist." Whatever! This is my top-secret notebook, and I can write anything I want!

T. T.
+
T. T.

The only thing we can't do together is talk about fairy godparents. It's hard not being able to tell my friends about them, but I know Da Rules.

Anyway, thanks to Cosmo and Wanda, A.J., Chester, and I have had some pretty wild adventures. One time they created the ultimate video game for us to actually become a part of. I had to rescue the guys from it before they got vide-o-bliterated! Sometimes having fairy godparents is a lot of hard work.

Speaking of hard work, no one works harder than my favorite comic book superhero, THE CRIMSON CHIN! And sometimes I'm right there by his side fighting crime and keeping Chincinatti safe as CLEFT, THE BOY CHIN WONDER! I even get my very own utility cleft!

And while we're talking superheroes, my mom and dad know a little bit about fighting for truth, justice, and the safety of planet Earth, ever since I wished for them to have superhero alter egos. I just wanted them to have more time in their day to do everything they needed to do and not get so tired doing it. But even without the alter egos my mom and dad are all right (as far as parents go.) Luckily for me, they don't ask too many questions, and when they do, they pretty much believe anything I say. . . .

When they turn into MIGHTY MOM and DYNO DAD, they're unstoppable! Although it turns out that when they're off saving the world, they don't have much time to spend with me. Still, I guess it's pretty neat having parents who could save the world if they had to.

Funny, even with all those superpowers, their supersenses still didn't clue them in to the fact that I had fairy godparents. . . .

We made sure of that, Timmy!

Sometimes I wonder what other people might wish for if they were lucky enough to get their own fairy godparents . . . hmmm, just imagine . . .

VICKY: To rule the world!

THE CRIMSON CHIN: Justice, thy name is chin!

FRANCIS: Duh?

TOOTIE: For Timmy's undying love, so when I chase him he'd actually let me catch him and I could kiss him all the time!

CROCKER: To discover the existence of Timmy Turner's FAIRY GODPARENTS! . . . and maybe some shrimp puffs.

A.J.: To fight aliens alongside CRASH NEBULA!

CHESTER: Yeah! And to be able to watch CRASH NEBULA all the time on TV!

A.J.: Wait, don't we already do that?

CHESTER: Who cares? It's cool!

A.J.: Also, to get our initials on the high-score screens of all the video games down at the arcade!

CHESTER: Yeah! And for, uh, world peace.

MOM: Well, of course, there's no such thing as fairy godparents, but if there were, we'd wish for lots of time to spend with our darling son, Timmy. . . .

DAD: And an all-expense paid vacation getaway to someplace warm and exotic with lots of sand and pineapples!

MOM: Right! We'll even pay Vicky overtime to watch Timmy!

Hey! I don't like this fantasy anymore.

Wish List!

What if YOU had fairy godparents? What would you wish for? Make a list! But remember to be careful what you wish for . . . some things aren't as much fun as they sound. Just ask Cosmo about the time I wished for a Super Toilet!

Finally, if I could wish anything for Cosmo and Wanda, I'd grant them a vacation. They sure need one!

Okay, time to put the book away. And remember, this is my top-secret, absolutely NOT-at-all-about-my-fairy-godparents notebook, so you're not going to tell anyone anything that I've just told you, right?

Go away now, nothing special to see here . . .

Didn't you hear me? Come on, before this book falls into the wrong hands, put it down!

. . . HEY! you're still here? Okay, well, I was hoping it wouldn't come to this, but:

I WISH YOU WOULD CLOSE THE BOOK AND WHEN YOU DO YOU'LL HAVE NO MEMORY OF MEETING ANY FAIRY GODPARENTS.

TREYACH

See ya!